WELCOME TO —THE— WOOFMORE

WELCOME TO
THE
WOOFMORE

BY DONNA GEPHART & LORI HASKINS HOURAN

ILLUSTRATED BY JOSH CLELAND

AMULET BOOKS • NEW YORK

Cataloging-in-Publication Data has been applied for and may be obtained from the Library of Congress.

ISBN 978-1-4197-6762-3

Text © 2024 Donna Gephart and Lori Haskins Houran
Illustrations © 2024 Josh Cleland
Book design by Natalie Padberg Bartoo

Printed and bound in China
10 9 8 7 6 5 4 3 2 1

Amulet Books are available at special discounts when purchased in quantity for premiums and promotions as well as fundraising or educational use. Special editions can also be created to specification. For details, contact specialsales@abramsbooks.com or the address below.

Amulet Books® is a registered trademark of Harry N. Abrams, Inc.

ABRAMS The Art of Books
195 Broadway, New York, NY 10007
abramsbooks.com

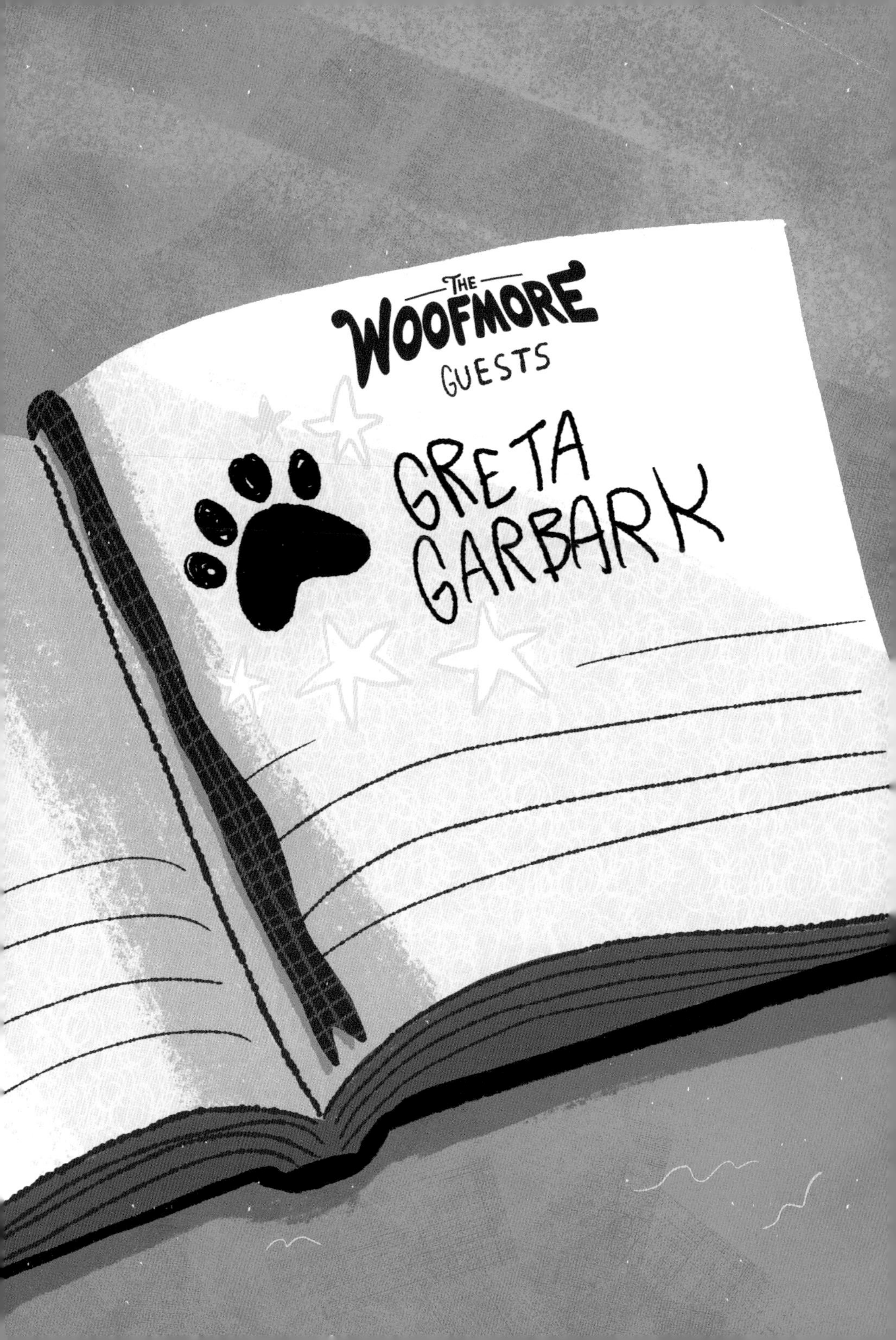
THE
WOOFMORE
GUESTS
GRETA
GARBARK

CHAPTER 1
GRAND OPENING

Rufus tugged his jacket. He fixed his bow tie. He smoothed his fur.

The boss, Ms. Coco, was coming!

Everything at the hotel had to be *paw*fect. Even him!

Ms. Coco's nails tapped across the marble floor. *Clickety-click. Clickety-click.*

"Good morning, ma'am," Rufus said.

"Hello, Rufus," said Ms. Coco.

She looked him over from nose to tail. It took a while. He was five times her size, at least.

Ms. Coco smiled. "*Paw*fect."

Phew!

"This is it," she said. "The grand opening of the Woofmore hotel! Is there a full water bowl in every room?"

"Yes, ma'am."

"A piece of kibble on every pillow?"

"Yes, ma'am."

"Good boy!"

Rufus wagged his tail. He liked being called a good boy.

3

"Now, Rufus, listen closely."

Rufus tilted his head. That was how he did his best listening.

"A VIP guest is arriving. As you know, *every* dog is a Very Important Pooch here at the Woofmore. But this guest is extra special."

"Extra special?"

Rufus made a little toot. *Oops!* Sometimes he did that when he felt nervous.

Ms. Coco did not notice.

"Please meet her limo, Rufus. And give her tip-top treatment all week."

"Yes, ma'am. Tip-top treatment!"

Ms. Coco clickety-clicked back to her office.

Who could the special guest be? Rufus didn't have to wait long to find out.

Crrrrrunch. A long white car pulled up the gravel driveway. The VIP!

Rufus hurried outside. He ran in two quick circles to calm himself. Then he opened the back door of the shiny limo.

A silky golden retriever jumped out. She wore a huge straw hat and sunglasses.

Who was she?

Rufus remembered his job.

"Welcome to the Woofmore hotel," he said. "My name is Rufus."

"Thank you, Rufus," said the retriever.

Her voice!

Rufus knew that voice!

And he knew exactly who the dog was behind those sunglasses.

Greta Garbark, the biggest movie star in the world!

He wanted to let out an excited howl.

"Quiet," he whispered to himself.

"Yes, quiet," said Ms. Garbark. "That is just what I need. Peace and quiet."

"Then that is what you will have," said Rufus.

Suddenly, a pack of pups burst from the bushes. They started yelling and snapping pictures.

"Greta! Greta! Over here. Smile for the cameras!"

"Oh no!" Ms. Garbark cried. "The *pup*arazzi! They have found me!"

"Hurry!" shouted Rufus. "Inside!"

CHAPTER 2

PEACE AND QUIET

ufus rushed Ms. Garbark into the hotel. He shut the doors behind them.

"You are safe," Rufus said. "They can't *hound* you in here."

"Just one problem," said Ms. Garbark.

She pointed her paw at some dogs in the lobby. Dozens of dogs. They were all checking in to the hotel.

"If they know who I am, I will not have peace and quiet. I will have a ruckus, Rufus."

Rufus wanted to do a good job. He wanted to give Ms. Garbark tip-top treatment.

Rufus did *not* want a ruckus.

"Do not worry. I have an idea," he said. "A *paw*fect idea."

Rufus called Sparkles from the Sudsy Spa on the second floor.

"Bring Ms. Garbark right in," said Sparkles. "We will take good care of her."

Ms. Garbark got a sudsy bath.

She got a fresh new *fur*style.

She got a bold new color—Pupster Purple. Nobody at the Woofmore would know who she was! Unless . . .

"What do you think?" Ms. Garbark asked Rufus.

"Shhhh!" he said.

"*Excuse* me?"

"Sorry!" said Rufus. "It's your voice. If the guests hear it, they will know who you are right away."

"I see. If I want quiet, I must *be* quiet."

"Yes," said Rufus.

Ms. Garbark closed her mouth.

She joined the other guests—quietly.

She dog-paddled in the pool. She lay in the sun. She read a magazine with her own picture on it.

No one knew who she was!

Rufus checked on Ms. Garbark. "Do you have peace? Do you have quiet?"

Ms. Garbark smiled. She gave him a big *paws*-up.

Rufus went to Ms. Coco's office. He told his boss about Ms. Garbark's spa disguise.

"Great job!" said Ms. Coco. She tossed Rufus a treat.

Rufus wagged his tail. He *was* doing a great job!

The special guest was happy. Everything at the hotel was *paw*fect.

The grand opening was going off without a hitch!

CHAPTER 3

A HITCH (AND AN ITCH)

Every day, Rufus checked on Ms. Garbark.
Every day, she gave him a big *paws*-up.
Every day, Ms. Coco tossed Rufus a treat.

Rufus would be sad to see Ms. Garbark leave tomorrow. He liked her. And he liked treats.

"Ms. Coco?" Hank the Housekeeper knocked on Ms. Coco's door. "We have a problem."

Rufus made a little toot. Problems made him nervous.

"The guest from Room 201 was scratching," said Hank.

"Scratching?" asked Ms. Coco.

"Scratching," said Hank. "The guest from Room 410 was scratching, too."

Ms. Coco looked out the window. She saw three guests at the pool. Three scratching guests!

"*No!* It can't be!" cried Ms. Coco. The fur on her back stood straight up. "Fleas. We have FLEAS at the Woofmore!"

Rufus tooted. A big one this time.

"What are we going to do?" asked Hank the Housekeeper.

Ms. Coco paced back and forth. *Clickety-click. Clickety-click.*

"There is only one answer," she said. "We must give every guest a flea bath. I will tell Sparkles to get ready."

Ms. Coco put her head in her paws. "This will ruin us. The Woofmore will be called a fleabag hotel!"

"Wait," said Rufus. "Let me think. Maybe there is a way to keep our good name!"

"Think fast, Rufus," said Ms. Coco. "We need to solve this problem today."

Bzzzzt! Bzzzzt! A buzzer sounded on Ms. Coco's desk.

"It's the VIP room," she said.

"Ms. Garbark needs something," said Rufus. "I will take care of it."

Ms. Coco groaned. "Ms. Garbark! When she finds out, we will be *finished*!"

Rufus hurried to the elevator.

Ding! The door opened. He stepped aside so two guests could get off.

"I hope you are enjoying your stay at the Woofmore," he said politely.

"Yes, it's lovely here!" said a poodle in pearls. She scratched her head.

"The food is terrific," said a husky in a hat. He scratched his chin. "We are heading to breakfast now."

Rufus got in the elevator. He pressed 10 for the top floor.

Ding! Rufus ran out. He tapped on Ms. Garbark's door.

"It's Rufus. May I help you?"

Ms. Garbark opened the door. "Hi, Rufus! Could I get—"

She stopped. "You look strange. What's wrong?"

"Nothing," said Rufus. "I'm fine."

But Rufus was not fine. Something was crawling on him.

Up his back. Up his shoulder. Up his neck.

Ms. Garbark said, "All right then. I just wanted—"

"*Ouch!*" Rufus felt a sharp bite on his ear.

"Rufus?"

Then it came—the feeling. The awful, hot, itchy feeling.

"Are you *sure* you're OK?"

His ear! It was SO. VERY. ITCHY.

Rufus couldn't take it anymore. He reached up his paw. *Scratchscratchscratch!*

"You, too?" said Ms. Garbark. "Why is everyone at the hotel scratching?"

"What—what do you mean?" asked Rufus. *Scratchscratchscratchscratchscratch!*

Ms. Garbark gasped. "It's *fleas*, isn't it?"

Oh no! Ms. Garbark knew!

The Woofmore was finished. And it was all his fault!

Rufus whimpered. His tail drooped.
But Ms. Garbark patted his shoulder.
"Do not worry. I have an idea," she said.
"A *paw*fect idea!"

CHAPTER 4
A RUCKUS

ufus followed Ms. Garbark to the dining room. It was full of guests having breakfast. They were chewing and chatting.

Ms. Garbark cleared her throat.

"Ladies and gentle*mutts*, may I have your attention, please?"

The guests stopped chewing. The guests stopped chatting.

Her voice!

They knew that voice!

"It's Greta Garbark!" cried the poodle in pearls. "The world's biggest movie star!"

"Only, she's *purple*," said the husky in a hat.

"That's right," said Ms. Garbark. "Don't you adore my new *fur*style? I got it right here, at the Sudsy Spa."

She posed with her paws on her hips.

"*Ooooh!*" said the guests. "*Aaaah!*"

"You can get a new style, too. The spa has a Greta Garbark special—today only! I will be there. You can get your picture taken with me."

The guests jumped up. They wanted the Greta Garbark special!

Rufus called Sparkles at the Sudsy Spa.

"Bring them right in," she said. "We will take good care of them!"

Each guest got a sudsy bath.
(With Flea-Be-Gone shampoo.)
Each guest got a fresh new *fur*style.
Each guest got a bold new color. They all chose Pupster Purple!

And each guest got a photo with Ms. Garbark. The dogs crowded around her. Dozens of dogs.

"This is a ruckus," whispered Rufus. "I'm sorry, Ms. Garbark."

Ms. Garbark smiled. "It's OK, Rufus."

While the pups were pampered, Hank the Housekeeper sprayed all the rooms with Flea-Be-Gone.

Then he got his own flea bath. So did Ms. Coco and Rufus and Sparkles. Ms. Garbark, too.

"The Woofmore is now flea-free," Ms. Coco said. "Thank you, Ms. Garbark."

"Thank *you*. I had a wonderful week. Lots of peace and quiet."

Then Ms. Garbark sighed. "I do not want to face the *pup*arazzi tomorrow."

"Maybe you do not have to face them," Rufus said.

"Im*paw*ssible!" Ms. Garbark said. "They always sniff me out."

"Do not worry. I have an idea," said Rufus.

"Let me guess, Rufus. A *paw*fect idea?"

Rufus grinned. "*Fur* sure."

CHAPTER 5

PUPSTER PURPLE

Rufus tugged his jacket. He fixed his bow tie. He smoothed his fur.

Ms. Coco stood beside him.

"Thank you for staying at the Woofmore," she told Ms. Garbark.

"Please come again," added Rufus.

"Oh, I will," promised Ms. Garbark. "Thank you so much for this." She pointed her paw at the guests in the lobby. Dozens of dogs, all waiting to help.

"Ready, everyone?" called Ms. Coco.

"Ready!" everyone answered.

Ms. Coco phoned the driver to bring Ms. Garbark's limo.

Crrrrrunch. The long white car pulled up in front of the hotel.

Ms. Garbark waved goodbye to Rufus and Ms. Coco. Then she walked out. But she wasn't alone. She was with all the other dogs. Dozens of dogs!

"Greta! Greta Garbark!"

The *pup*arazzi burst from the bushes.

"Greta? Where are you? *Greta*?"

The *pup*arazzi could not spot her! There were too many pups. Too many purple pups!

Rufus watched out the window. He saw Ms. Garbark slip into the back of her limo. He saw her ride away—in peace and quiet.

Rufus wagged his tail.

"What a week!" said Ms. Coco.

"It was a bit *ruff*," said Rufus. "But we made it."

Ms. Coco gave Rufus an extra big treat. "Enjoy your day off. Next week, we will have our *second* special guest at the Woofmore!"

Second VIP? Oh, boy.

Rufus couldn't help it. He tooted.

Twice!

ABOUT THE AUTHORS AND ILLUSTRATOR

Lori Haskins Houran and **Donna Gephart** are longtime *fur*ends who love books, dogs, and books about dogs! They had a *paw*some time writing this one. Lori lives in Massa*chihuahua*-setts and Donna hails from *Chew* Jersey. Get more de*tails* at lorihaskinshouran.com and donnagephart.com.

Josh Cleland is an illustrator working out of his home studio just outside of Portland, Oregon, where he resides with his wife, Rayna, and creative director/dog, Newman. His work has been featured in various children's magazines, including *Highlights* and *Storytime*, as well as on greeting cards, billboards, and more.

CHECK BACK IN TO
THE WOOFMORE WITH BOOK 2,
THE WOOFMORE IS NOT *HAUNTED.*
COMING SOON!